Disney

Finding Tinker Bell

a Never Girls adventure

beyond
never land

written by Kiki Thorpe

illustrated by Jana Christy

A STEPPING STONE BOOK™

RANDOM HOUSE 🏠 NEW YORK

For Abigail
—K.T.

Library of Congress Cataloging-in-Publication Data is available upon request.

ISBN 978-0-7364-3599-4 (trade) — ISBN 978-0-7364-8182-3 (lib. bdg.) —
ISBN 978-0-7364-3650-2 (ebook)

rhcbooks.com

Printed in the United States of America

10 9 8 7 6 5 4 3 2 1

This book has been officially leveled by using the F&P Text Level Gradient™ Leveling System.

Far away from the world we know, on the distant Never Sea, lies an island called Never Land. It is a place full of magic, where mermaids sing, fairies play, and children never grow up. Adventures happen every day, and anything is possible.

Though many children have heard of Never Land, only a special few ever find it. The secret, they know, lies not in a set of directions but deep within their hearts, for believing in magic can make extraordinary things happen. It can open doorways you never even knew were there.

One day, through an accident of magic, four special girls found a portal to Never Land right in their own backyard. The enchanted island became the girls' secret playground, one they visited every chance they got. With the fairies of Pixie Hollow as their friends and guides, they made many magical discoveries.

But Never Land isn't the only island on the Never Sea. When a special friend goes missing, the girls set out across the sea to find her. Beyond the shores of Never Land, they encounter places far stranger than they ever could have imagined. . . .

This is their story.

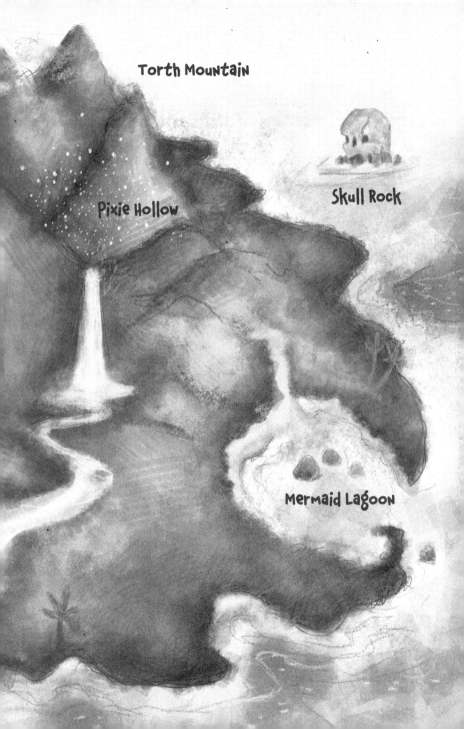

chapter 1

The box sat on a high shelf, peeking out from behind a stack of old magazines. It was a plain brown box, dusty with neglect. It looked no different from a dozen other boxes in the basement, and yet six-year-old Gabby Vasquez was sure she'd never noticed it before.

Gabby turned to her older sister, Mia, who was lying on the couch with her nose stuck in a book.

"What's in there?" Gabby asked, pointing at the box.

Mia glanced up. "Junk, probably," she said with a sulk. Mia was in a bad mood. It was the first Saturday of summer, and the sisters' plans to go swimming had been spoiled by a sudden rainstorm. Instead of splashing in the pool with their friends, they had spent the morning moping around the house and squabbling over the remote control. At last, in exasperation, their mother had sent them both down to the basement to get them "out of her hair."

As Mia went back to reading, Gabby looked around the room. An old wooden chair sat in the corner. Gabby grabbed it and dragged it noisily over to the shelf. Mia watched her over the top of her book.

Gabby climbed onto the chair and reached for the box. Even on her tiptoes, she couldn't quite touch it.

She climbed off the chair and found a pillow. She put the pillow on the chair, stepped on top of it, and reached for the box again. Beneath her, the chair wobbled.

With a loud sigh, Mia set her book down. "For Pete's sake, Gabby, don't hurt yourself. *I'll* get it."

Mia climbed onto the chair and took down the box, which was taped tightly shut. Someone had written across the top in fat black marker.

Gabby knew all her letters, but sometimes she still had trouble with long words. "What does it say?" she asked.

"'Treasure,'" Mia read. "'Handle with care.'"

The girls raised their eyebrows at each other. "I'll get the scissors!" Gabby exclaimed. She raced up the stairs and hurried down a moment later with the kitchen shears. Mia reached for them, but Gabby held the scissors out of her grasp. "I get to open it. I saw it first!"

"Careful, Gabby." Mia hovered over her

sister as she sliced through the packing tape and pulled open the flaps.

The box was full of crumpled yellowed newspaper. The girls eagerly began to dig through it.

"I've got it—oh." Mia lifted something from the box, then sat down with a disappointed sigh. "It's only an old boat."

"Only" isn't the right word, Gabby thought. True, the little wooden boat wasn't fancy. Its green paint was chipped and faded, and it didn't have a lot of sails or a dragon-shaped prow or anything else grand. It was just a humble little fishing boat, with a squat cabin, a single sail, and a net made out of string. Even its name was funny. *Tino's Treasure* was painted on the side in wobbly, uneven letters.

But Gabby sensed something special

about it right away. "Let me see," she said, reaching for the boat.

The moment it was in her hands, a shiver ran through her. She felt as if the boat were waiting for something.

An adventure, maybe, Gabby thought.

"There's got to be something else in here." Mia fished through the newspaper still inside the box. Gabby knew she was hoping to find jewelry or some elegant keepsake. Mia loved pretty things.

"Oh . . . look!" Mia pulled out a small gold-handled magnifying glass. She held it up to her eye, like a detective, and peered at Gabby's face. "Aha! A clue! From your mustache, I conclude that you had milk for breakfast."

Gabby giggled. "Where'd this stuff

come from?" she asked her sister.

"I don't know," Mia said. "Let's ask Papi."

They went upstairs and found their father in the living room, working on his laptop. "Papi, look at this." Gabby held up the boat.

When Mr. Vasquez saw the boat, his eyes widened. "The *Treasure*! My gosh, I haven't seen this in years!" He took it gently in his hands, smiling as if at an old friend. "I thought it was lost. Where on earth did you find it?"

"In the basement," Gabby told him.

"This, too." Mia held out the magnifying glass.

"Abuelo's old magnifying glass," their father said warmly.

"This belonged to *Grandpa*?" Gabby couldn't believe it. Their grandfather was a stern, grumpy man. When they visited, he spent most of his time watching television and grumbling about the news. Gabby couldn't imagine him ever playing with such a wonderful toy.

"No," their father said. "This belonged to *my* abuelo, your *great*-grandfather. He loved model ships. Look." Mr. Vasquez took the magnifying glass and held it up to the fishing net. "See the detail? All those knots were done by hand. And these." He pointed out the rubber tires hanging on the side. "These bumpers came off an old toy car. I used to spend hours playing with this. I pretended it was my boat, and imagined all the adventures I could have."

Gabby had been imagining that, too. "Papi, can I play with it?"

Her father hesitated, but only for a second. "Of course, *mija*. But be careful. It's special to me."

"I will. I promise." Gabby gently took the boat. She made it rock up and down, as if it were sailing on the sea.

The doorbell rang. Their father got up to answer it.

"Hi, Mr. Vasquez," said two familiar voices.

Gabby and Mia both ran to the door. Their friends Kate McCrady and Lainey Winters stood on the doorstep. Water streamed from their raincoats.

"Can Mia and Gabby come out to play?" Lainey asked. She was trying to use her wet sleeve to wipe the raindrops off her big round glasses, rather unsucessfully.

"In this weather?" Mr. Vasquez asked with a frown.

Kate's broad white smile flashed beneath her hood. "Oh, don't worry, Mr. Vasquez," she assured him. "We won't be out in the rain for long."

The girls exchanged secret looks. They all knew what Kate meant. They were going to Never Land! A portal to the magical island lay behind a loose fence board in Mia and Gabby's backyard. The four girls had discovered it together, and they used it to travel to Never Land whenever they could.

"Please, Papi. Just for a little bit," Gabby begged.

"All right," he said. "But come inside

right away if you see lightning."

"We will!" the sisters said in unison.

Kate and Lainey waited on the doorstep while Gabby and Mia scrambled into their raincoats. Gabby was halfway to the door when she spied the model ship on the coffee table. She grabbed it, tucked it under her raincoat, and ran after the other girls.

Chapter 2

In Pixie Hollow, the fairy Tinker Bell
stared out the window of her teakettle
workshop. Outside, a warm wind was
blowing. The wind was strong. It bent the
buttercups, rattled the meadow grass, and
made the cart mice jumpy.

The wind blew down the chimney
spout of the kettle, making a loud whistle,
but Tink didn't notice. She was watching
a butterfly outside.

The butterfly struggled against the

wind. Its wings fluttered and flapped desperately, but it wasn't getting anywhere. Tink felt sorry for it.

At some point, though, the butterfly seemed to stop struggling. It spread its wings and let the wind carry it. Up, up it soared. Tink leaned out the window to watch it as it became a small dot of yellow against the treetops. Then it was an even smaller dot against the blue sky.

Tink couldn't see the butterfly anymore, but still she stayed with it. In her mind, *she* was the butterfly, flying high above Never Land, higher than she'd ever gone. She could see beyond Never Land, across the sea, all the way to the edge of the world, where the sky was pink and purple and gold and even some colors she'd never seen before. She could—

"Tinker Bell. Tink? *Tink!*"

Tinker Bell snapped out of her reverie. Her friend Bobble the sparrow man was standing in the doorway of her workshop. He held a large, greasy black pot in his skinny arms. He frowned at Tink with concern.

"Oh! Fly with you, Bobble," Tink greeted him. Traces of her daydream clung like cobwebs to the corners of her mind. She shook her head to clear them. "What have you got there?"

"Dulcie's pot is giving her trouble again," Bobble said. "It keeps turning her chocolate mousse into gooseberry jelly.

She sent it to be tinkered. Asked for you specifically."

"I'll take a look at it," Tink replied. "You can leave it there."

Bobble set the pot down with a grunt of relief. "That pot's got a mind of its own. I swear it made itself heavier the whole way here. I keep telling Dulcie she ought to have someone make her a new one, but she won't hear of it. Says she's attached to the old thing."

"That's okay," Tinker Bell said. "I like a challenge."

Tink turned to her worktable. But Bobble continued to stand in the doorway, blinking at her through his glasses. They were made from two dewdrops held in place by wire frames, and they made his eyes look enormous. It was hard not to notice him staring.

"Is there something else?" Tink asked.

Bobble cleared his throat. "Erm . . . if you don't mind my asking, are you feeling all right?"

"Yes," Tink answered. "Why?"

"It's just that you don't seem yourself lately," Bobble said.

"I'm all right," Tink replied, rubbing her forehead. "I think I just have a bit of island fever."

"Fever?" Bobble's brow furrowed. "Should I call a nursing fairy?"

"No, not that kind of fever." Tink sighed and looked out the window again. "Bobble, don't you ever get the urge to fly beyond Never Land?"

Bobble shook his head. "Can't say that I do."

"Sometimes I just feel . . . I don't know, like I'm missing something. Maybe there's more I could be doing than just fixing pots and pans."

"It's the south wind," Bobble told her firmly. "It's been blowing hard lately. You've got to be careful when the wind blows from the south. Strange things are bound to happen. It can put odd notions in your head."

"Hmm. Maybe," said Tink. She didn't believe that south-wind nonsense.

"Well." Bobble peered at her carefully. "You're sure you're all right?"

Tink gave him a reassuring smile. "Yes, Bobble. I'm perfectly fine."

"Just let me know if you need anything." Bobble closed the door behind him.

When he was gone, Tink turned to Dulcie's pot. It wasn't the first time she'd had to fix it. Bobble was right about the pot having a mind of its own. No matter which ingredients the baking fairy used, the pot only cooked what *it* felt like making.

It was just the sort of problem Tink usually liked. But today her heart wasn't in it. She examined the pot for a few moments, then set it aside.

From beneath her worktable, Tink pulled out a map. She unrolled it across the table, weighing the corners down with her tinker's hammer and pots of glue. The map was made of birch bark so old it was starting to yellow. She had to take extra care that the edges didn't crumble.

In the center of the map was a drawing of Never Land, but that didn't interest Tink. She knew Never Land like the back of her hand. What caught her eye were words scribbled off to the side. Someone had written in faint, spidery handwriting:

Shadow Island

What was Shadow Island? Tink had been wondering ever since she found the map in the Home Tree library, shoved behind a shelf of books about caterpillar farming. She had crossed the sea dozens of times on adventures with Peter Pan, but she'd never seen Shadow Island. She'd never even heard of it.

Tink squinted at the map. She could see other lines overlapping the drawing. They were smudged and faint, as if someone had drawn something there, then erased it.

Like a shadow, Tink thought.

A spark of an idea had grown in Tink's mind. If there really was a Shadow Island, maybe she could be the fairy to find it.

But how? A fairy could fly only so

far before her wings gave out. Of course, she could ask her old friend Peter Pan to come—he could carry her when she got too tired. But Peter was unreliable. One minute he'd be there, the next he'd be off chasing eagles or playing with mermaids. Tink knew she couldn't count on him.

"Bah!" said Tink, rolling up the map. Why was she wasting her time with mysteries and maps? She was a tinkering-talent fairy, and her place was here, in Pixie Hollow. Goodness knows she had plenty to do.

Tink went back to working on Dulcie's pot. She'd just located the source of the problem—a patch of rust was making the pot surly—when she heard a whistle.

Her ears pricked up. This time it wasn't

the wind whistling in her chimney spout. It was a reed whistle. It sounded once, twice.

With a gasp, Tink let go of the pot and fluttered into the air. The whistle was a scout's alarm. A fairy was in trouble!

chapter 3

Gabby and the other girls had almost reached the Home Tree when they heard the whistle. It was a thin piping sound, faint, but urgent, coming from across the meadow.

From all over Pixie Hollow, fairies came fluttering. They emerged from the tiny doorways that lined the Home Tree's branches and dropped their thimble buckets and pine needle brooms to the ground. They left behind their herds of caterpillars and field mice and flew toward the meadow.

"What's happening?" Mia called out to a fairy as she darted past.

The fairy barely paused. "It's a scout's alarm. Someone needs help!"

A fairy was in trouble! Gabby set down her great-grandfather's boat between the roots of the Home Tree and ran after the fairies. The other girls were right behind her.

They followed the whistle all the way through the meadow to the orchard on the far side. The orchard was usually one of Gabby's favorite places in Pixie Hollow. Plum, apple, and cherry trees grew there, and the grass was soft and green. Gabby loved to lie in the shade of an apple tree and watch harvest-talent fairies buzz back and forth, picking ripe fruit.

But today the orchard was still. The harvest fairies hovered next to their trees. They looked as if they were under a spell. As other fairies flew into the orchard, they stopped, too, and stared at something on the ground.

At first Gabby didn't see it. As she ran forward, Mia suddenly grabbed her arm and pulled her back. "Gabby, watch out!"

Then Gabby saw. A snake lay in the tall grass. It was long and green and as thick around as a jump rope. A few feet away, a lone fairy cowered at the base of a tree.

The whole orchard seemed frozen. Everyone watched the snake. The snake watched the fairy.

Slowly, the snake lifted its head and tested the air with its tongue.

"Why doesn't the fairy fly away?" Gabby whispered.

"I don't think she can," Kate whispered back. "She's too scared. She has no glow." The fairy's glow had gone out completely. She looked no brighter than a mouse.

"She's afraid to move," Lainey agreed. "A snake can strike much faster than a fairy can fly."

Two animal-talent fairies, Fawn and Beck, had flown as close to the snake as they dared. They were talking to it in low voices. Gabby hoped they were telling it to go away.

But the snake took no notice of them. It seemed to be in a trance. Its head swayed a

little, and its tongue flickered again.

Gabby couldn't stand it. "Somebody *do* something!" she begged.

Out of the corner of her eye, she saw Kate's hand creep into the air and twist an apple off the tree above them.

Kate's wrist snapped forward, lightning quick.

The apple struck the ground right in front of the snake, startling it. The snake coiled in on itself.

The movement broke the spell in the orchard. Two scouts swooped in and whisked the petrified fairy away. Other fairies flew at the snake, shouting and clacking pebbles together.

The girls joined in making a racket. They stomped their feet and hollered. They banged sticks together.

The snake coiled tighter. It looked annoyed. There went its lunch, and now all the noise was making things worse.

As the clamor grew, the snake decided it had had enough. It uncoiled and slithered away.

The fairies and the girls cheered. Fairies swarmed around Kate. They pinched her cheeks and patted her head. The air rang with their praise.

Kate blushed beneath her freckles. "It was just a fastball," she said.

The terror of watching the fairy, followed by the burst of relief, made Gabby feel fizzy with energy. As they

followed the fairies back to the Home Tree, she couldn't stop talking. "Kate, that was so neat. You threw that apple *so* fast. I want to learn to throw like that. Will you teach me? Promise?"

Kate laughed. "I'd be glad to teach you, Gabby."

"And I helped scare away the snake, too!

I stomped my feet really hard. I think that helped!"

"It definitely did," Lainey agreed.

"That fairy was really scared," Gabby babbled on. "I think we should do something nice for her. Like maybe we could pick some flowers for her. Or make something— I know! We can make her a card! It can say 'We hope you feel better soon.' I can even draw a picture on it!"

Mia grinned. "That's a great idea, Gabby."

They walked on, Gabby bursting with energy and ideas. She passed right by her great-grandfather's little wooden boat without even noticing it.

chapter 4

Tink flew slowly back to her workshop. The rescue had gone well, but she felt gloomy. She thought about how small and vulnerable fairies were. A flying fairy wouldn't make it far on her own. Seeing the petrified fairy in the orchard had only been a reminder of that.

I wish there were some other way, she thought.

Tink drew up short. She hovered in the air, staring.

A boat sat in a clump of flowers not two feet from her workshop door. It was a big, sturdy boat, with a sail made of cloth.

A Clumsy's boat, Tink thought. Yet it was the perfect size for a fairy.

Tink turned to see who the boat belonged to, but there wasn't a Clumsy in sight. The boat looked as if it had dropped straight out of the sky and landed there in her buttercups.

Tink fluttered over to it. The moment she stepped onto the deck, she sensed the boat was special. Tink knew about making things. She could tell when something was well crafted, and she knew when something had been made with love. This boat was both.

All of a sudden, Tink understood—

her wish had been granted! She was sure Never Land had something to do with it. The magic of Never Land could never be underestimated.

Of course, when magic gives you a gift, you have to take it.

Getting the boat inside the teakettle was the hardest part. The doorway to

Tink's workshop was only three inches tall, and the boat was a good deal bigger. Tink managed it at last, though it took nearly a gallon of fairy dust to magically squeeze it through.

Once the boat was inside, Tink got to work. She sealed all the cracks with pine tar and waterproofed them with beeswax. She patched the sail. The lines were made of plain old cotton string, so she replaced them with good, fairy-made rope. She oiled the ship's wheel and checked the rudder.

The cabin was musty, so she gave it a good airing, then moved her own bed in. She added a soft thistledown comforter and a pussy-willow pillow so she'd be cozy during cold nights at sea.

Last but not least, Tink tinkered a shiny new brass bell. She engraved the boat's name on the side, changing just one letter so it read *Tink's Treasure*.

When she rang the bell, its peal was deep and satisfying.

Tink worked for three days and nights, but at last the boat was ready. The sun was setting as she stepped back to admire it. She thought it was the finest boat she'd ever seen, even better than the grand ships anchored in Pirate Cove.

She had one more thing to do—she needed a map. Of course, she had the one under her desk. But it was a *library* map. She couldn't just take it.

Tink sat down and spread out a piece of onionskin. She would trace the map and return the original to the library.

She had just started tracing the map onto the papery skin when she heard a knock on her door.

Tink opened it. Four of her friends stood on the doorstep—Iridessa, the light fairy; Fawn, the animal fairy; Rosetta, the garden fairy; and Silvermist, the water fairy. They looked at Tink gravely.

"All right, Tinker Bell. What's going on?" Iridessa demanded.

"What do you mean?" Tink asked.

"We know you're up to something," Iridessa replied. "We haven't seen you for days. You've missed every meal—"

"There are candles burning in your workshop all night long," Rosetta added.

"The dust-keepers say you've used

buckets of fairy dust," Silvermist said.

"Yeah," Fawn agreed. "Something *stinks* around here."

There was a pause. Rosetta wrinkled her nose and whispered, "Er, Fawn, I think that might be you."

"Me?" Fawn sniffed her shirt. "Oops. I ran into a stinkbug today. Boy, was *he* in a mood."

Iridessa rolled her eyes. "Tink, what we're trying to say is, we think you're hiding something from us."

"I'm not hiding anything," Tink replied, stepping aside. "Come in and see for yourselves."

Her friends crowded through the doorway, then stopped and stared. Tink had magically stretched the inside of her workshop to make room for the boat, but it still took up most of the room.

"It's a boat," Silvermist observed.

"A *big* boat," Rosetta added.

"You're not going to turn pirate on us, are you, Tink?" Fawn asked.

Tink laughed. "Of course not! I just want to sail it."

"*What?*"

"*Where?*"

"*When?*"

"*Why?*" her friends asked all at once.

"On the Never Sea, of course," Tink answered. "If the weather's right, I'll leave tomorrow. As for why—well, simply because I can."

Her friends stared at her in amazement. Rosetta placed a gentle hand on her arm.

"Tink, honey, are you feeling all right?"

"I feel fine," Tink said. "Why does everyone keep asking me that?"

"It's just . . . why a *boat*?" Silvermist asked. "You aren't even a water fairy."

"So?" Tink tugged on her bangs, which she did when she was annoyed. She hadn't expected so many questions. "I know my way around a ship. I've been on plenty of pirate ships with Peter Pan."

"Ah! So you're going with Peter!" said Iridessa. The others nodded, as if they finally understood.

"No," Tink said, tugging harder. "This has nothing to do with him."

That was mostly true, but not completely. Journeys with Peter had given Tink her first real taste of adventure. And as any true adventurer knows, adventures are like chocolate ice cream or Never Berry pie. Once you've gotten a taste, you always crave more.

But this time, Tink didn't need Peter. She could have an adventure on her own. "Haven't you ever wanted to do something really *big*?" she asked her friends.

"Sure," said Iridessa. "That's when I make a rainbow—"

"Or a waterfall—" said Silvermist.

"Or a tree grow—" added Rosetta.

"Or a lion roar," said Fawn. "You don't have to leave Never Land to do something big."

"Well, maybe I want to be different. Maybe I want to be the first fairy to sail across the Never Sea," Tink said. "I might even discover something new." She was about to add *like Shadow Island,* but then she thought better of it. Instead, she said, "You're my friends. Aren't friends supposed to support one another's dreams?"

Her friends looked abashed. "Of course I support you, Tink," Silvermist said quickly.

"Me too."

"So do I."

"We all do," said Iridessa. The fairies wrapped their arms around Tink and pulled her into a hug.

"But you have to promise to come back," Rosetta added.

Tink laughed. "I promise."

She said good-bye to her friends. After they left, she went back to tracing the map.

The faint shadow lay offshore, to the east of Never Land, so that was where Tink decided to start. She used a hummingbird quill dipped in blackberry ink. The coast of Never Land was easy to trace—the line showed firmly through the onionskin. But

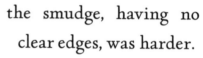

the smudge, having no clear edges, was harder.

Tink turned up the lantern. As she bent over her work, the bright light cast her shadow on the rounded wall of her teakettle workshop.

Scritch, scritch, scritch.

Tink's quill scratched across the page. On the wall, her shadow's quill moved, too. She reached to dip the quill in the inkwell, and her shadow did the same.

It had been a long day. The workshop was warm and cozy. Soon, Tink's eyelids grew heavy. The quill slipped from her hand.

And yet, from the corner of her eye Tink seemed to see her shadow still working. A dark island appeared on the map where before there had been none.

Ah, so that's Shadow Island, Tink thought sleepily.

Huh?

Tink's eyes flew open. She grabbed the map and held it up to the light.

Nothing was there.

"I'm imagining things," she said with a laugh. She set down the map, then yawned and stretched her arms. On the wall, her shadow yawned and stretched, too.

"I'll finish in the morning," Tink said, reaching over and turning down the lantern. Then she started for the door.

In the dim light, she didn't notice that her shadow remained where it was, bending over the map.

Chapter 5

"Gabby," Mr. Vasquez said, "where is the boat?"

Gabby was sitting at the kitchen table in her house, drawing a picture of Never Land. She paused while coloring a mermaid's tail and looked up. "What boat, Papi?"

"Great-Grandpa's boat, the one you found in the basement," he said. "What did you do with it?"

"Ohhhh. *That* boat!" Gabby set down her

crayon so she could think. She'd taken the boat to Pixie Hollow . . . and then what? Gabby searched her mind, but she couldn't remember where she'd put it. "I know it's . . . somewhere."

"Did something happen to it?" her father asked with a frown.

"No!"

"Then where is it?"

"Um . . . ," said Gabby.

Her father looked at her for a long moment. Then he sat down at the table. "*Mija,* I know that boat looks like an old toy, but it's important to me—"

"I know," Gabby interrupted. "I was *very* careful. It's just that—"

Her father held up a hand. "No, listen. I haven't told you *why* it's important. You see, your great-grandfather made it."

"He *made* it?" said Gabby. No wonder the boat seemed so different from other toys!

"With his own hands," her father said. "He was a wonderful craftsman. I loved watching him work. He made all kinds of things—wooden animals, dollhouse furniture—but the boat was always my favorite. I think he would have liked to sail a boat like that. When I was old enough, he gave it to me. It's the only thing of his that I still have. And you've been careless with it."

Gabby's throat felt tight. She saw now that she *had* been careless. For the first time, her father had trusted her with something important, and she'd let him down. It was an awful feeling to have.

"I'll find it, Papi," she choked out. "I promise I won't come back without it."

Gabby ran from the kitchen up to her room. The boat was there somewhere. It had to be!

She dug through her toy box and looked in her closet. She pulled everything out from under her bed. She found three socks, seven barrettes, an old school art project, and thirty-seven cents—but no boat.

Gabby was digging through her dresser drawers when Mia passed by in the hall. She stopped in the doorway of Gabby's room and stared. "What are you doing?"

"I can't find the boat!" Gabby cried.

"What boat?" asked Mia.

"Great-Grandpa's boat. From the

basement," Gabby said. "I think it's lost."

Mia sucked in her breath. "Uh-oh. Is Papi mad?"

"No..." Gabby shook her head tearfully. She almost wished her father *were* mad. Being disappointed in her was so much worse. "I have to find it."

"We will." Mia put her arm around her sister. "Let's just retrace your steps. Where was the last place you saw it?"

"In Pixie Hollow," Gabby said. "I was bringing it to show the fairies. I thought maybe I could give them a ride."

"And then what happened?" asked Mia.

Gabby thought hard. "And then ... and then ... Oh! I know! I set it down when we all ran to help save that fairy from the snake. It must still be there." She started for the door. "We have to go to Pixie Hollow right now!"

"I'll get Kate and Lainey," Mia said, heading for the phone. The four girls had a rule that they would never go to Never Land without one another.

Twenty minutes later, the friends had gathered by the loose fence board.

"I can't stay for long," Lainey said. "My mom says I have to be home in a half hour to help with dinner."

"We'll just find the boat and come back," Mia told her. "Anyway, you know time never really passes when we're all together in Never Land. You'll be home in plenty of time."

"Let's go rescue that boat!" Kate patted Gabby's shoulder.

Gabby gave her a weak smile. The achy feeling in her throat had gone away. She was glad Kate and Lainey were there. They would help her find the boat, and soon she'd be placing it back in her father's hands. *I'm proud of you for taking care of it,* she imagined him saying.

"Come on," Gabby said. She pushed the fence board aside and crawled through.

The first moments of stepping into Pixie Hollow were always the most magical. The ground changed from stubbly grass to soft, springy moss. The sounds of cars and lawn mowers were replaced by the jingle of fairy laughter. Even the air felt enchanted—it smelled like orange blossoms and sparkled with dust from the wings of passing fairies.

But this time, Gabby hardly noticed any of it. She crossed Havendish Stream in two bounds and raced up the hill to the Home Tree. Mia, Lainey, and Kate were right behind her.

Together, the girls searched by the tree. But the boat was nowhere around.

"Are you sure this is where you left it?" Lainey asked.

"Yes," Gabby said. She pointed to a patch of flowers not far from Tink's workshop. "I set it right there."

"Maybe the fairies moved it," Mia said. "Let's ask someone. Excuse me!" She flagged down a passing fairy.

The fairy paused in midair. She was wearing the walnut-shell cap of a fruit harvester. A pair of cherries hung over her shoulder. "Yes?"

"I'm looking for my boat. I left it here. Maybe you've seen it? It's green and about this big—"

The fairy shook her head. "Haven't noticed any boats. Why not check the dock? That's where I'd look."

"Good idea!" said Kate. The girls

returned to Havendish Stream and followed it down to the bend where the fairy boats were docked. They saw tiny birch-bark canoes, boats with leaf-sails, and rafts made of twigs. But Mia and Gabby's great-grandfather's boat wasn't among them.

"What if I never find it?" Gabby asked.

"Don't give up," Kate told her. "Let's ask Tink. The boat was right outside her workshop. Maybe she'll know what happened to it."

When they got to Tink's teakettle, Gabby knelt down and gently tapped her finger on the metal door. No one answered. She tried to look in the windows, but the curtains were drawn.

Should she knock again? She knew

Tink didn't like to be bothered when she was working.

At that moment, Fawn flew by carrying an armload of sunflower seeds. She stopped when she saw the four girls crouched outside Tink's workshop.

"Tink's gone," she said.

They all turned to look at her. "What do you mean, 'gone'?" Mia asked.

"She found a boat, a nice big sturdy one," Fawn explained. "She went out to sea in it this morning. You just missed her."

Chapter 6

Out at sea, Tinker Bell took a deep breath of ocean air. The sun was shining and the blue sky stretched wide above her. The strong south wind, which had been so bothersome in Pixie Hollow, was now at her back, speeding the *Treasure* along.

A wave rose in front of the boat. Tink gripped the wheel as the *Treasure* climbed it, then dove down the leeward side. The waves out here were bigger than she'd thought they would be. Flying above them, she'd always thought they looked so small. But Tink felt sure the boat was sturdy enough to ride them.

Still, to be on the safe side, she had sprinkled the sail with fairy dust so the *Treasure* could fly when needed. In case of emergency, a little magic never hurt.

Up and down the boat went, riding the swells. Skull Rock loomed ahead. Tink checked her onionskin map. She was right on course and making good time.

Suddenly, Tink's heart leaped. A long, silver-blue shape slid through the wave below her. Something was under the boat!

With a splash, a fish shot out of the water. It sailed over the *Treasure* and kept on flying, its pink fins spread out like wings. The tip of its tail traced graceful arcs on the water.

Tink had barely recovered from the surprise when a second fish leaped out. It spread its fins and soared after its friend. In a moment, fish were leaping all around the boat. She was caught in a school of flying fish!

The fish were almost as big as the boat. But Tink wasn't afraid. With a whoop, she let out the sail again. As the wind caught it, the *Treasure* lifted, helped by the fairy dust. In seconds, she was soaring along next to the fish.

The fish dove back into the water. But a moment later they leaped up and flew alongside her. They seemed to want to play, too!

The school of fish banked right, and she followed them. She was flying so close, she could feel spray flying off their fins. Tink waved at one of them from the deck. It was hard to say for sure, but she thought the fish waved back.

Tink didn't know how long she followed the fish. They'd been flying for some time, when all of a sudden, as if led by some hidden cue, the fish dove back into the water and disappeared.

Tink steered the boat downward and landed with a splash. She looked for Skull Rock to get her bearings.

She couldn't see the skull-shaped cave anywhere. Had she passed it without even noticing?

The wind had grown stronger. The

Treasure rose and plunged on the choppy waves.

Tink knew she needed to get to calmer waters. But Never Land was well behind her now. Did she dare sail on?

She studied the map. If she was where she thought she was, Shadow Island should be close. Tink looked in every direction, but all she could see was water and sky.

As Tink scanned the horizon, she noticed a single dark cloud ahead. It looked out of place in the bright blue sky.

Strange. I didn't notice it before, Tink thought.

But she didn't have time to dwell on it. Suddenly, a wave caught the boat and nearly turned it over. By the time she righted it, Tink knew she couldn't risk sailing on. She needed to head back to

Never Land before it was too late.

She turned the *Treasure* around, but she was fighting against the wind now. She crossed wave after wave, but land didn't seem to be getting any closer. Her only choice was to get off the water and try to fly the boat back through the air.

Tink had just started to tack, angling the sail, when she noticed the cloud right above her. Was it her imagination, or was the cloud following her?

"That's silly," Tink said aloud. The cloud would go where the wind went, of course, and the wind was against her. At any rate, she didn't have to worry about a storm. There was only the one small cloud—all around it, the sky was blue.

No sooner did she have that thought

than she felt the air turn cold. A raindrop splashed down on the *Treasure's* deck. Another followed.

For a fairy, a rainstorm is no small thing. Each drop is enough to soak her. What to a human would be a light sprinkle felt to Tink like standing under a waterfall.

Tink dodged raindrops as they spattered down. She ran for the cabin but slipped on the wet deck, and one of her pompom

slippers fell off. She tried to grab it, but the boat pitched and it rolled away. She gave up chasing after it and ran for cover.

Inside the cabin, Tink peered out at the rain. Great drops battered the deck. But strangely, she could see that just beyond the curtain of rain, the ocean was calm. Sunlight sparkled on its surface. The *Treasure* seemed to be caught in a miniature storm. If she could just sail through it, she'd be safe.

Just then, a blast of wind hit the boat so hard the sail broke loose. The sheet flapped uncontrollably, like a hand waving for help. Tink ran to catch it but was too late.

With a shuddering jerk, the boat rose into the air. She heard the howl of a gale.

The wind seemed alive, like a creature that had caught the boat and was tossing it around like a plaything.

The ship's bell clanged wildly as the boat began to spin faster and faster. Tink grabbed the railing and held on tight. Light flashed around her as she was pulled up, up, up . . . into the dark cloud.

chapter 7

Gabby stood on the beach near Pixie Hollow, looking out to sea. The glare on the water hurt her eyes, but she couldn't stop staring. She pointed to something out on the waves.

"There! See that? Is it Tink?"

Mia, Lainey, and Kate squinted at the far-off dot. "I think it's just a pelican," Kate said.

Gabby's shoulders slumped. They'd been

waiting for ages on the beach. But there was still no sign of Tink or *Tino's Treasure*.

Mia gave her shoulder a squeeze. "Don't worry. I'm sure Tink won't let anything happen to the boat."

"But when will she be back?" Gabby cried. "We've been waiting all day!"

"Let's check with Fawn," Lainey suggested. "Maybe one of the seagulls has spotted her."

When Gabby had explained to Fawn that Tink had taken *her* boat and she needed it back, Fawn had gone to the shorebirds. She asked them to keep an eye out for a fairy in a boat. With luck, they could get a message to Tink to sail back as soon as possible.

The girls found Fawn farther down the

beach, talking to a big gray seagull. The four friends knelt beside her. "Any news?" Kate asked.

Fawn shook her head. "He just came back from Skull Rock, but he didn't see any sign of Tink or the boat. Don't worry," she added, when she saw Gabby's face. "Tink can take care of herself. Back in the days when she'd go off with Peter Pan, she'd sometimes disappear for a dozen full moons. But she always came back."

A dozen full moons! Gabby couldn't wait that long. "But I need the boat back *now*," she insisted.

"Maybe we should go home for a little while," Lainey suggested. "The next time we come to Pixie Hollow, Tink will be back. Anyway, I have to get home to help with dinner. My mom asked me to shell the peas."

Peas? Gabby thought. *Who cares about peas?* Tink had taken her great-grandfather's one-of-a-kind boat and sailed off to who knows where, and all Lainey could talk about was peas!

Gabby folded her arms across her chest. "I promised Papi I wouldn't come back without Great-Grandpa's boat," she told them. "I'm not going home until I have it."

The three older girls stared at her. Gabby narrowed her eyes and glared back until Lainey held up her hands in surrender.

"All right, Gabby," she said with a sigh. "Have it your way. We'll wait."

"There's no use just sitting around on the beach." Kate stood and brushed the

sand off her pants. "Why don't we find something else to do? When Tink gets back, I'm sure we'll hear about it."

Gabby wouldn't have minded waiting on the beach. But she followed the other girls back up the trail to Pixie Hollow.

As they passed the Home Tree, Gabby noticed Tink's teakettle workshop. Maybe it was just the way the sunlight came slanting through the tree branches. But for a second, Gabby imagined she saw a wisp of smoke rise from the chimney spout.

A sudden hope seized her. Maybe Tink wasn't really out at sea. Maybe she'd hidden the *Treasure* as a joke. She imagined Tink inside her teakettle, waiting for someone to find her so they could laugh about her trick together.

As the other girls walked ahead, Gabby stopped. She knelt down and tapped on the door with her finger. When there was no answer, she gave it a little push. The door opened easily.

The doorway was so small Gabby had to lie flat on the ground to see inside. It was a bit like looking into a sugar egg, the kind where you peep through a hole onto a miniature scene.

The teakettle's rounded walls were lined with shelves that held Tink's tools— tiny pliers, bitty pots of paint and glue, and scraps of steel wool no bigger than Gabby's pinkie fingernail. A rocking chair made from a human-sized spoon sat in one corner, next to a lamp with a tea-strainer shade. A potholder rug covered the floor.

The fire poker was made from an old silver toothpick.

But the fire was cold. Tink wasn't there.

The lump returned to Gabby's throat. Where had Tink gone? And what was Gabby going to tell her dad?

She was about to get up when she spied something on Tink's worktable that looked like a note. Gabby's hand was too big to fit through the doorway, so she used a twig to fish it out.

It wasn't a note—it was a map! Right away, Gabby knew it was important.

The map fit into the palm of her hand. She could see writing on it, but it was too small for her to read. But she knew who could!

Folding the map gently into her fist, Gabby raced after her sister and their friends.

"Look!" she shouted. "Look what I found!"

The other girls turned. Gabby held up the map.

Kate took it from her. "What's this?"

"A clue!" Gabby said excitedly. "I found

it in Tink's workshop. It's a mop."

Mia gave her a disapproving look. "Tink wouldn't like it if she knew you were snooping in her workshop."

Gabby ignored her. "Do you still have Great-Grandpa's magnifying glass?" she asked.

Mia took the magnifying glass from her pocket and peered at the map. "What's Shadow Island?" she asked after a moment.

"I've never heard of it," said Lainey. "Let me see." She took the magnifying glass and studied the map. "It's weird. It says Shadow Island right here, but I only see Never Land on the map."

"I bet that's where Tink went!" Gabby exclaimed.

"I don't know, Gabby," Mia said. "It's just a drawing. It might not mean anything."

A bird screamed above them. Gabby looked up. A seagull was flying toward them, carrying Fawn on its back. The water-talent fairy Silvermist was with her.

The seagull descended and landed at the girls' feet. Fawn fluttered off.

"What happened? Did you find Tink?" Gabby asked.

"Not exactly." Fawn had a strange look on her face. She glanced at Silvermist. "A plover found this tangled in some seaweed."

Fawn held out her hand. She was holding Tink's pompom slipper!

Chapter 8

The girls stared at the tiny green shoe. The little ball of fluff was wet and bedraggled. It barely looked like a shoe at all. But Gabby knew it was Tink's slipper. She had never seen her without them.

"So what? It's just her shoe," Kate said after a moment. "Maybe it fell off."

"Maybe she got tired of wearing shoes and kicked them overboard," Mia added.

"Sure," said Silvermist uncertainly.

Gabby was only half listening. *I was the one who brought the boat to Pixie Hollow,* she thought. *Tink's in trouble because of me.* The lump in her throat was back. It felt as big as a hard-boiled egg.

"Fawn sent out more seagulls to look for her," Silvermist told the girls. "Fawn and I will go, too."

"Tink's probably fine," Fawn added quickly. "But . . . we want to be sure."

Gabby swallowed hard around the lump. "I'm coming with you," she said.

The fairies looked at each other. Gabby could tell they didn't like the idea.

"It's cold out at sea," Fawn replied. "We may have to fly far, and there won't be anywhere to rest. Maybe it's better if you stay here."

Gabby folded her arms across her chest again. This time, she wasn't going to let anyone tell her what to do.

"It's my boat—well, I'm the one who lost it, anyway. Besides, I'm the one who found the clue."

"What clue?" asked Fawn.

Lainey held out the map. "Gabby found this in Tink's workshop. What is Shadow Island?"

"Never heard of it," said Fawn.

"I have." Silvermist looked over Fawn's shoulder. "It's a mysterious island where nothing is as it should be. But it's just a story. It's not a real place."

"See, I told you, Gabby," Mia said.

"We didn't know Never Land was real either until we found it," Gabby replied.

Kate raised her eyebrows. "She has a point."

Mia sighed. "Well, if Gabby's going with you, then we all are."

Fawn nodded. "All right. It will be a search party. Go to the mill and ask the dust-keepers for extra fairy dust, and something to carry it in. You'll need a lot. We don't know how far we'll have to fly."

"We'll round up other fairies and meet back here," Silvermist said.

As the other girls set off for the mill, where the fairy dust was stored, Gabby studied the map. Shadow Island didn't look like an island at all, only a vague smudge out in the sea. It was hard to tell anything about it, even exactly where it was.

Then Gabby had a brainstorm so good

that she stood right up. She could ask Spinner!

Spinner was a story-talent sparrow man who traveled far and wide, searching for stories that he spun into magical tales. Once, he'd even traveled home with Gabby, hiding in her backpack so he could learn more stories at her school.

If anyone could tell her about Shadow Island, it was him.

Finding Spinner was the problem. He came and went from Pixie Hollow, and no one ever seemed to know where he was or how long he'd be gone. When he was home, he liked to relax in the oddest places. He'd once told Gabby that he found it impossible to sleep indoors, since he'd spent so much time under the stars.

Gabby looked all over Pixie Hollow. She had almost given up, when she found him, dozing inside a water lily in the watering hole where the cart mice drank.

When Gabby woke him, Spinner sat up and yawned. His patched cap sat crookedly on his head, and the toes sticking out of his shoes looked cold. But he grinned when

he saw her. "Well, if it isn't my favorite honorary fairy. Fly with you, Gabby."

"Hi, Spinner," Gabby said. "I've been looking all over for you. I was afraid you were gone."

"I just got back from Torth Mountain last night," Spinner told her. "Long journey. Wore me out. Luckily, I found this nice water bed." He patted the lily.

"It's pretty," Gabby said.

"And very comfortable," Spinner said. "I was having the most marvelous dream about a flying pink tiger. Would you like to hear it?"

"Not now," Gabby said quickly. Spinner's stories were extraordinary— they transported the listener and made you feel as if you were there. But Gabby didn't have time to listen to a story. "I have a question."

When she showed him the map, Spinner nodded. "Oh, Shadow Island. Now, there's a strange place."

"So it's real!" Gabby said.

"I didn't say that," Spinner replied. "Never been there myself. But I've heard stories about it."

"What kind of stories?" Gabby asked.

"Spooky tales—stories about creatures who live their whole lives in darkness. Giants who touch the sky. Talking deserts. That sort of thing."

Gabby shivered. Shadow Island didn't sound like a place she wanted to go.

"Do you know how to get there?" she asked Spinner.

Spinner shook his head. "No one does. I've been looking for it my whole life, but I've never found it. They say you can only reach the island if it wants to be found."

"Like Never Land," Gabby said.

"Aye." Spinner took a bit of straw from his cap and chewed the end. "Can I ask why you're so interested in it?"

"Tink's gone, and she took my boat," Gabby told him. "I need it back. I think maybe she was going to Shadow Island."

"Oh." Spinner frowned.

"What?" asked Gabby.

"Well," Spinner said. "There's one thing I do know. Anyone who has ever reached Shadow Island has never made it home to tell about it."

"Never?" repeated Gabby.

Spinner shook his head.

Now Gabby was no longer just worried about her boat—she was worried about her friend.

Chapter 9

Weak sunlight shone through the windows of the *Treasure* and made yellow patches on the walls and floor.

Inside the cabin, Tinker Bell slowly got to her feet. The boat had finally stopped spinning and tossing. She could still hear the ocean outside, but now the waves made a quiet *shush-shush* noise.

Cautiously, Tink opened the cabin door and peeked out. The wind had died down.

The storm was over. There was no sign of the cloud that had carried her off.

She stepped all the way out and saw that the *Treasure* had run aground on a beach. The tide had gone out, and the boat was stuck in the wet sand.

Tink's foot felt cold. She looked down and remembered she had lost a shoe. She searched the entire boat, but she couldn't find it.

"It must have blown away in the storm," Tink said. It was her favorite shoe, too— her pompom slipper.

Tink kicked off her other shoe—there was no point in wearing just one—and turned her attention to the boat. The paint was worn away where the wind and rain had battered it. The sail was ripped, but that didn't worry her. She would enjoy patching it.

When Tink turned to the mast, she stared. A crack ran right across it. Unless it was fixed, she wouldn't be able to fly the boat, much less sail it home.

A smile spread slowly across Tink's face. She loved to fix things. And this was a problem worthy of her skills!

Tink's stomach rumbled. She realized

she hadn't eaten since she'd left Pixie Hollow earlier that day—or had it been the day before? The sun was low on the horizon, but Tink couldn't say for sure whether it was morning or evening.

She decided she'd have a good meal, then get started on fixing the boat.

Not knowing how long she'd be gone, Tink had brought plenty of food—fresh bread, wheels of cheese, thimble buckets of honey, and dried cherries. She took a cherry and ate on the deck while she thought about what to do.

She figured the storm had blown her back to Never Land. But though she'd been to every corner of the island, the beach here didn't look familiar. She didn't know which way Pixie Hollow was, or how far.

By the time she had finished breakfast, the sun was no higher in the sky. In fact, it seemed not to have moved at all.

Tink looked again. No, it *had* moved, but not in the expected way. It seemed to have shifted to the right. Tink had the strange impression that rather than climbing to its zenith, the sun was slowly moving around the island, like a wolf circling at a distance. She felt as if she was being watched.

Of course, Never Land was known to do strange things. It could move about on the waves, or stretch itself so the horizon changed. But she'd never seen this before.

Tink stood and took a deep breath. Yes—adventure was in the air.

She decided the mast could wait. First,

she would go exploring. After all, hadn't the whole point of this journey been to discover something new?

She refreshed her fairy dust from a barrel belowdecks. One cupful was all a fairy needed for a day of flying, but Tink took a second cupful, put it in a pouch, and tied it to her belt, just in case.

She started out over the sand, flying toward the dense forest that grew just inland. She hadn't gotten far, though, when she again had the feeling she was being watched. Tink turned.

Nothing there—only her own shadow on the sand.

"Jumpy, aren't we?" she said to herself, her voice sounding loud in the silence.

She flew on and had almost reached the

edge of the forest when she thought she saw something move out of the corner of her eye.

Tink spun around. But it was only her shadow again. The low angle of the sun made it stretch long across the sand. She looked like a giant!

Tink had never imagined herself as a giant before. She waved her arms and spun in the air. She fluttered her wings double-time. The giant shadow Tink danced along with her.

Tink twirled around again. She was still spinning when she saw another shadow fall next to her own. She turned to see who it belonged to.

No one was there.

When she turned to look back at the shadows, she saw that a third one had joined in.

Tink's heart leaped, then dropped. Suddenly, she understood why the sun looked so different, and why the beach was so unfamiliar.

She wasn't on Never Land. She wasn't *anyplace* she'd ever been before.

And she wasn't alone.

chapter 10

When Gabby got back to the beach, Mia, Kate, and Lainey were waiting. Kate had a large sack of fairy dust and was doling out pinches to the other girls.

"Here you go, Gabby." Kate sprinkled fairy dust over her. Gabby felt a familiar tingle and her toes floated a little off the ground.

Fawn was saddling two seagulls, while Silvermist looked on. Gabby was surprised to see Iridessa and Rosetta there as well.

"We're joining the search party," Iridessa explained. "Tink's our friend, too."

"Don't call it a search party," Silvermist said. "It sounds so . . . serious."

"But that's what we're doing," Iridessa said. "We're *searching* for Tink."

"We're *looking* for Tink," Silvermist corrected. "Tink, our friend who has just gone for a quick boat trip and will probably be back any moment. After all, we don't know that anything is wrong."

Iridessa frowned and opened her mouth to reply, but Rosetta cut her off. "Searching, looking—who cares? We just want to be sure she's okay," she said.

"Right," said Fawn, cinching a saddle tighter. The seagull shifted and ruffled its wings. "The gulls are ready. Silvermist, you and I will ride *Aaawrk*." Fawn squawked the name with a seagull accent. "Rosetta, you and Iridessa take *Cawwr*."

Rosetta eyed the large seagull. "I'm not riding that bird."

"Why not?" asked Fawn.

"He smells like fish," Rosetta complained. "And I don't like the way he's looking at me."

Fawn rolled her eyes. "Of course he smells like fish. He's a seagull. It's windy at sea, Ro. You won't make it far flying on your own. You'll get blown away like dandelion fluff."

Rosetta put her hands on her hips. "Then I'll ride with one of the girls."

"I'll carry you. I don't mind," Gabby

volunteered. She loved holding fairies, but they rarely allowed it.

"There, see?" Rosetta fluttered over and landed on Gabby's shoulder. It tickled, but in a nice way. She settled herself and took hold of Gabby's collar. "All set."

The slight weight of Rosetta on her shoulder made Gabby feel better. Her

talk with Spinner had left a twisty feeling in her stomach. She'd learned nothing about Shadow Island—nothing helpful, anyway.

But the other fairies didn't seem worried, and their mood rubbed off on Gabby. Maybe everyone was right. Maybe Shadow Island was just a made-up place after all. Gabby hoped so.

"What should I do with this?" she asked, holding up the map.

"Hold on to it, I guess," Silvermist told her. "I don't know how much use it will be, though, since I still don't believe the island exists." She looked around. "Everyone ready?"

"Look!" Mia said suddenly, pointing.

A small dark cloud had appeared on

the horizon. It was all by itself in the bright blue sky. It reminded Gabby a little of a lost black sheep.

"It's only a cloud," Fawn said, shrugging. "Nothing to worry about."

Fawn and Silvermist climbed onto their seagull, and Iridessa got on hers. The gulls spread their wings and lifted off.

One by one, the girls rose after them— Kate first, followed by Mia and Lainey.

Gabby took a deep breath of the salty air and pushed off the ground. She didn't feel worried anymore. She was going to find Tink and the *Treasure* and bring them home. She was sure of it. And she knew her friends would help her every step of the way.

Read this sneak peek of
through the dark forest,
the next **Finding Tinker Bell**
adventure

. . .⋆ ⋆⋆ . ⋆ . . .

Of all the strange, magical things that happened to her on Never Land, the one thing Mia Vasquez could not get used to was flying.

Each time the fairy dust settled over her and she felt its magic—a tickly feeling, like soda bubbles rising inside her—Mia thought, *This time will be different. This time I won't be scared.* And for an instant, as her feet left the ground, it really would seem different. When she floated up, light as a leaf, everything seemed possible.

As soon as she was above the treetops, though, she started to panic. She had to close her eyes and take deep breaths. It was hard not to think about falling.

But what choice did she have? Flying was the only practical way to get around Never Land, especially in the company of fairies. So Mia had learned to hide her fear. Her best friends, Kate and Lainey, didn't know she was still afraid of flying. Neither did her little sister, Gabby. And she certainly didn't tell the Never fairies. Everyone thought Mia had simply gotten over her fear of heights, the way you get over a cold or a case of the hiccups.

The trick, she found, was never to look down. Mia kept her eyes on the horizon. She forced a calm expression onto her face. She had gotten so good at pretending she wasn't afraid that some days she even managed to convince herself.

Today, unfortunately, was not one of those days.

As she flew out over Never Sea, a knot formed in Mia's stomach. The cold ocean wind tangled her long hair. It raised goose bumps on her arms. Flying over land was hard enough. But flying above water was a thousand times worse. In every direction, all she could see were white-capped waves. Losing her nerve here was not an option.

Keep going, Mia told herself. *Think of Tink!*

Their fairy friend Tinker Bell was lost at sea in a little toy boat. Mia, Kate, Lainey, Gabby, and four fairies from Pixie Hollow had come out to search for her. But it was an impossible task. Looking for a toy boat in the vast Never Sea was like trying to spot a pinhead in a mountain of sand.

"See anything?" Kate called over the wind.

"Nothing yet," Mia yelled back. Looking for Tink meant looking down, and that was the one thing Mia couldn't do. "Do we even know this is the right way?"

Kate shook her head. "Tink could be anywhere."

It was all Gabby's fault. Mia glared at the back of her little sister's head. If Gabby hadn't left their great-grandfather's model boat in Pixie Hollow, Tinker Bell wouldn't have found it. And if Tink hadn't found the boat and taken it out sailing, they wouldn't be out here looking for her now.

As if she felt Mia's eyes on her, Gabby glanced over her shoulder. She reached out her hand, and Mia's anger softened. She couldn't blame Gabby for wanting to find the boat. Their father had been so upset when Gabby lost it. The *Treasure* was—well, a family treasure. Gabby had promised not to come home without it.

What their father didn't know was they'd lost it in Never Land. The magical island was the girls' secret.

Mia sped up and caught Gabby's hand. It felt small and warm in her own cold one. She told herself that she was comforting her sister, not the other way around.

Two seagulls, carrying the fairies Fawn, Iridessa, and Silvermist, came circling back toward the girls. The fourth fairy, Rosetta, was riding on Gabby's shoulder.

"Let's turn around!" Iridessa shouted. The wind almost carried her voice away.

But Mia heard her. Relief spread through Mia's chest.

"We can't stop looking!" Gabby piped up. "Tink's still out here somewhere!"

"I don't think she could have come this far. Not in such a small boat," Silvermist said.

"We won't stop," Fawn reassured Gabby. "But we don't know which way Tink went. We need to warm up and rest. Then we'll try another direction."

The group turned back toward Never Land, but the wind was against them now. Mia felt as if someone were holding her shoulders, trying to push her backward. Ahead, she could see Never Land's shore, with its thin white thumbnail of sand. Only a few more minutes and her feet would be on the ground.

Abruptly, the air grew colder. Mia looked up and saw a dark cloud had moved across the sun.

They had seen the same cloud earlier. Mia was sure of it. From the ground, it had seemed little and harmless, a distant smudge in the bright blue sky. But up here, in the air, it looked bigger and darker.

A raindrop splashed against Mia's face.

The search party stopped and treaded air. They were at the edge of the storm. Ahead, rain hung like a curtain between them and Never Land.

"We'd better not fly through it!" Fawn shouted from the back of her seagull.

"Let's take the long way around," Iridessa agreed. "We can fly north over the tip of the island and come in from the west."

Mia's heart sank. That would mean at least another hour of flying. Maybe more. And they were so close! "It's only a little rain," she argued.

"I don't like the look of that cloud," Rosetta said from Gabby's shoulder.

Mia saw her friends hesitate. If she didn't do something quickly, they'd agree to take the long route. "You guys fly around, if you want," she said with a boldness she didn't feel. "I'm going ahead." Without waiting for an answer, she plunged into the storm.

Behind her, Mia heard someone shouting her name, but she couldn't tell who it was. The cold raindrops stung her skin and blurred her vision. She could no longer see Never Land's shore. Was she even going in the right direction?

Mia paused to get her bearings. Then she made her worst mistake: she looked down.

At the sight of the choppy sea below, Mia's confidence fled. She dropped like a stone.

She screamed, but the sound was lost in the wind. The sea sped toward her. Mia braced herself for the cold water.

There came a blinding flash. The cloud above her blazed from within. The air frizzled with electricity.

And suddenly everything flipped. That was the only word Mia could think of to describe it. The world seemed to turn itself upside down.

A second later, she came down hard on dry sand.